A FLOWER·FAIRY ALPHABET

A FLOWER·FAIRY ALPHABET

Poems and pictures by

CICELY MARY BARKER

FREDERICK WARNE

FREDERICK WARNE

Published by the Penguin Group
Penguin Books Ltd, 80 Strand, London WC2R 0RL, England
Penguin Putnam Inc., 375 Hudson Street, New York, N.Y. 10014, USA
Penguin Books Australia Ltd, 250 Camberwell Road, Camberwell,
Victoria 3124, Australia
Penguin Books Canada Ltd, 10 Alcorn Avenue, Toronto, Ontario, Canada M4V 3B2
Penguin Books (NZ) Ltd, Cnr Rosedale and Airborne Roads, Albany,
Auckland, New Zealand
Penguin Books India (P) Ltd, 11 Community Centre, Panchsheel Park,
New Delhi 110 017, India
Penguin Books (South Africa) (Pty) Ltd, PO Box 9, Parklands 2121, South Africa

Penguin Books Ltd, Registered Offices: 80 Strand, London WC2R 0RL, England

Web site at: www.flowerfairies.com

First published 1934
First published by Frederick Warne 1990
This edition first published 2002
7 9 10 8

ISBN 0 7232 4832 X

Printed in China

CONTENTS

THE FLOWERS IN THIS BOOK

ENGLISH NAME	BOTANICAL NAME	NATURAL ORDER
Apple Blossom	Pyrus Malus	Rosaceæ
Bugle	Ajuga Reptans	Labiatæ
Columbine	Aquilegia Vulgaris	Ranunculaceæ
Double Daisy	Bellis Perennis	Compositæ
Eyebright	Euphrasia Officinalis	Scrophulariaceæ
Fuchsia	Fuchsia	Onagraceæ
Gorse (or Furze)	Ulex Europœus	Leguminosæ
Herb Twopence	Lysimachia Nummularia	Primulaceæ
Iris (wild)	Iris Pseudacorus	Iridaceæ
Jasmine	Jasminum Officinale	Oleaceæ
Kingcup (or Marsh Marigold)	Caltha Palustris	Ranunculaceæ
Lily-of-the-Valley	Convallaria Majalis	Liliaceæ
Mallow (common)	Malva Sylvestris	Malvaceæ
Nasturtium	Tropœolum	Geraniaceæ
Orchis (Early Purple)	Orchis Mascula	Orchidaceæ
Pansy	Viola Tricolor	Violaceæ
Queen of the Meadow (Meadow-Sweet)	Spiræa Ulmaria	Rosaceæ
Ragged Robin	Lychnis Flos-Cuculi	Caryophyllaceæ
Strawberry (wild)	Fragaria Vesca	Rosaceæ
Thrift	Armeria Maritima	Plumbaginaceæ
Vetch (Tufted)	Vicia Cracca	Leguminosæ
Wallflower	Cheiranthus Cheiri	Cruciferæ
Yellow Deadnettle (Archangel)	Lamium Galeobdolon	Labiatæ
Zinnia	Zinnia	Compositæ

Apple Blossom

THE SONG OF
THE APPLE BLOSSOM FAIRIES

Up in the tree we see you, blossom-babies,
    All pink and white;
We think there must be fairies to protect you
    From frost and blight,
Until, some windy day, in drifts of petals,
    You take your flight.

You'll fly away! But if we wait with patience,
    Some day we'll find
Here, in your place, full-grown and ripe, the apples
    You left behind—
A goodly gift indeed, from blossom-babies
    To human-kind!

THE SONG OF
THE BUGLE FAIRY

At the edge of the woodland
Where good fairies dwell,
Stands, on the look-out,
A brave sentinel.

At the call of his bugle
Out the elves run,
Ready for anything,
Danger, or fun,
Hunting, or warfare,
By moonshine or sun.

With bluebells and campions
The woodlands are gay,
Where bronzy-leaved Bugle
Keeps watch night and day.

B

Bugle

Columbine

THE SONG OF
THE COLUMBINE FAIRY

Who shall the chosen fairy be
 For letter C?
There's Candytuft, and Cornflower blue,
Campanula and Crocus too,
Chrysanthemum so bold and fine,
And pretty dancing Columbine.

Yes, Columbine! The choice is she;
 And with her, see,
An elfin piper, piping sweet
A little tune for those light feet
That dance among the leaves and flowers
In *someone's* garden.
 (Is it ours?)

THE SONG OF
THE DOUBLE DAISY FAIRY

Dahlias and Delphiniums,
  you're too tall for me;
Isn't there a *little* flower
  I can choose for D?

In the smallest flower-bed
Double Daisy lifts his head,
With a smile to greet the sun,
You, and me, and everyone.

Crimson Daisy, now I see
You're the little lad for me!

D

Double Daisy

Eyebright

THE SONG OF
THE EYEBRIGHT FAIRY

Eyebright for letter E:
Where shall we look for him?
Bright eyes we'll need to see
Someone so small as he.
Where is the nook for him?

Look on the hillside bare,
Nibbled by bunnies;
Harebells and thyme are there,
All in the open air
Where the great sun is.

There in the turf is he,
(No sheltered nook for him!)
Eyebright for letter E,
Saying, "Please, this is me!"
That's where to look for him.

THE SONG OF
THE FUCHSIA FAIRY

Fuchsia is a dancer
Dancing on her toes,
Clad in red and purple,
By a cottage wall;
Sometimes in a greenhouse,
In frilly white and rose,
Dressed in her best for the fairies' evening ball!

(This is the little out-door Fuchsia.)

F

Fuchsia

G

Gorse

THE SONG OF
THE GORSE FAIRIES

"When gorse is out of blossom,"
    (Its prickles bare of gold)
"Then kissing's out of fashion,"
    Said country-folk of old.
Now Gorse is in its glory
    In May when skies are blue,
But when its time is over,
    Whatever shall we do?

O dreary would the world be,
    With everyone grown cold—
Forlorn as prickly bushes
    Without their fairy gold!
But this will never happen:
    At every time of year
You'll find one bit of blossom—
    A kiss from someone dear!

THE SONG OF
THE HERB TWOPENCE FAIRY

Have you pennies? I have many:
    Each round leaf of mine's a penny,
Two and two along the stem—
    Such a business, counting them!
(While I talk, and while you listen,
    Notice how the green leaves glisten,
Also every flower-cup:
    Don't I keep them polished up?)

Have you *one* name? I have many:
    "Wandering Sailor", "Creeping Jenny",
"Money-wort", and of the rest
    "Strings of Sovereigns" is the best,
(That's my yellow flowers, you see.)
    "Meadow Runagates" is me,
And "Herb Twopence". Tell me which
    Show I stray, and show I'm rich?

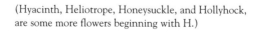

(Hyacinth, Heliotrope, Honeysuckle, and Hollyhock,
are some more flowers beginning with H.)

H

Herb Twopence

I

Iris

THE SONG OF
THE IRIS FAIRY

I am Iris: I'm the daughter
Of the marshland and the water.
Looking down, I see the gleam
Of the clear and peaceful stream;
Water-lilies large and fair
With their leaves are floating there;
All the water-world I see,
And my own face smiles at me!

(This is the wild Iris.)

THE SONG OF
THE JASMINE FAIRY

In heat of summer days
With sunshine all ablaze,
Here, here are cool green bowers,
Starry with Jasmine flowers;
Sweet-scented, like a dream
Of Fairyland they seem.

And when the long hot day
At length has worn away,
And twilight deepens, till
The darkness comes—then, still,
The glimmering Jasmine white
Gives fragrance to the night.

J

Jasmine

Kingcup

THE SONG OF
THE KINGCUP FAIRY

Golden King of marsh and swamp,
Reigning in your springtime pomp,
Hear the little elves you've found
Trespassing on royal ground:—

"Please, your Kingship, we were told
Of your shining cups of gold;
So we came here, just to see—
Not to rob your Majesty!"

Golden Kingcup, well I know
You will smile and let them go!
Yet let human folk beware
How they thieve and trespass there:

Kingcup-laden, they may lose
In the swamp their boots and shoes!

THE SONG OF
THE LILY-OF-THE-VALLEY FAIRY

Gentle fairies, hush your singing:
Can you hear my white bells ringing,
Ringing as from far away?
Who can tell me what they say?

Little snowy bells out-springing
From the stem and softly ringing—
Tell they of a country where
Everything is good and fair?

Lovely, lovely things for L!
Lilac, Lavender as well;
And, more sweet than rhyming tells,
Lily-of-the-Valley's bells.

(Lily-of-the-Valley is sometimes called Ladders to Heaven.)

L

Lily-of-the-Valley

M

Mallow

THE SONG OF
THE MALLOW FAIRY

I am Mallow; here sit I
Watching all the passers-by.
Though my leaves are torn and tattered,
Dust-besprinkled, mud-bespattered,
See, my seeds are fairy cheeses,
Freshest, finest, fairy cheeses!
These are what an elf will munch
For his supper or his lunch.
Fairy housewives, going down
To their busy market-town,
Hear me wheedling: "Lady, please,
Pretty lady, buy a cheese!"
And I never find it matters
That I'm nicknamed Rags-and-Tatters,
For they buy my fairy cheeses,
Freshest, finest, fairy cheeses!

THE SONG OF
THE NASTURTIUM FAIRY

Nasturtium the jolly,
   O ho, O ho!
He holds up his brolly
   Just so, just so!
(A shelter from showers,
   A shade from the sun;)
'Mid flame-coloured flowers
   He grins at the fun.
Up fences he scrambles,
   Sing hey, sing hey!
All summer he rambles
   So gay, so gay—
Till the night-frost strikes chilly,
   And Autumn leaves fall,
And he's gone, willy-nilly,
   Umbrella and all.

Nasturtium

Orchis

THE SONG OF
THE ORCHIS FAIRY

The families of orchids,
    they are the strangest clan,
With spots and twists resembling
    a bee, or fly, or man;
And some are in the hot-house,
    and some in foreign lands,
But Early Purple Orchis
    in English pasture stands.

He loves the grassy hill-top,
    he breathes the April air;
He knows the baby rabbits,
    he knows the Easter hare,
The nesting of the skylarks,
    the bleat of lambkins too,
The cowslips, and the rainbow,
    the sunshine, and the dew.

O orchids of the hot-house,
    what miles away you are!
O flaming tropic orchids,
    how far, how very far!

THE SONG OF
THE PANSY FAIRY

Pansy and Petunia,
  Periwinkle, Pink—
How to choose the best of them,
Leaving out the rest of them,
  That is hard, I think.

Poppy with its pepper-pots,
  Polyanthus, Pea—
Though I wouldn't slight the rest,
Isn't Pansy *quite* the best,
  Quite the best for P?

Black and brown and velvety,
  Purple, yellow, red;
Loved by people big and small,
All who plant and dig at all
  In a garden bed.

P

Pansy

Queen of the Meadow

THE SONG OF
THE QUEEN OF THE MEADOW FAIRY

Queen of the Meadow
where small streams are flowing,
What is your kingdom
and whom do you rule?
"Mine are the places
where wet grass is growing,
Mine are the people of marshland and pool.

"Kingfisher-courtiers,
swift-flashing, beautiful,
Dragon-flies, minnows,
are mine one and all;
Little frog-servants who
wait round me, dutiful,
Hop on my errands and come when I call."

Gentle Queen Meadowsweet,
served with such loyalty,
Have you no crown then,
no jewels to wear?
"Nothing I need
for a sign of my royalty,
Nothing at all but my own fluffy hair!"

THE SONG OF
THE RAGGED ROBIN FAIRY

In wet marshy meadows
A tattered piper strays—
Ragged, ragged Robin;
On thin reeds he plays.

He asks for no payment;
He plays, for delight,
A tune for the fairies
To dance to, at night.

They nod and they whisper,
And say, looking wise,
"A princeling is Robin,
For all his disguise!"

R

Ragged   Robin

S

Strawberry

THE SONG OF
THE STRAWBERRY FAIRY

A flower for S!
Is Sunflower he?
He's handsome, yes,
But what of me?—

In my party suit
Of red and white,
And a gift of fruit
For the feast tonight:

Strawberries small
And wild and sweet,
For the Queen and all
Of her Court to eat!

THE SONG OF
THE THRIFT FAIRY

Now will we tell of splendid things:
Seagulls, that sail on fearless wings
Where great cliffs tower, grand and high
Against the blue, blue summer sky.
Where none but birds (and sprites) can go.
Oh there the rosy sea-pinks grow,
(Sea-pinks, whose other name is Thrift);
They fill each crevice, chink, and rift
Where no one climbs; and at the top,
Too near the edge for sheep to crop,
Thick in the grass pink patches show.
The sea lies sparkling far below.
Oh lucky Thrift, to live so free
Between blue sky and bluer sea!

T

Thrift

UV

Vetch

THE SONG OF
THE VETCH FAIRY

Poor little U
Has nothing to do!
He hasn't a flower: not one.
For U is Unlucky, I'm sorry to tell;
U stands for Unfortunate, Ugly as well;
No single sweet flowery name will it spell—
Is there nothing at all to be done?
"Don't fret, little neighbour,"
   says kind fairy V,
"You're welcome to share
   all my flowers with me—
Come, play with them, laugh, and have fun.
I've Vetches in plenty for me and for you,
Verbena, Valerian, Violets too:
Don't cry then, because you have none."

(There are many kinds of Vetch; some are in the hay-fields,
but this is Tufted Vetch, which climbs in the hedges.)

THE SONG OF
THE WALLFLOWER FAIRY

Wallflower, Wallflower, up on the wall,
Who sowed your seed there?
                    "No one at all:
Long, long ago it was blown by the breeze
To the crannies of walls
    where I live as I please.

"Garden walls, castle walls, mossy and old,
These are my dwellings;
    from these I behold
The changes of years;
    yet, each spring that goes by,
Unchanged in my sweet-smelling
    velvet am I!"

W

Wallflower

XY

Yellow Deadnettle

THE SONG OF
THE YELLOW DEADNETTLE FAIRY

You saucy X! You love to vex
Your next-door neighbour Y:
And just because no flower is yours,
You tease him on the sly.
Straight, yellow, tall,—of Nettles all,
The handsomest is his;
He thinks no ill, and wonders still
What all your mischief is.
Yet have a care! Bad imp, beware
His upraised hand and arm:
Though stingless, he comes leaping—see!—
To save his flower from harm.

THE SONG OF
THE ZINNIA FAIRY

Z for Zinnias, pink or red;
See them in the flower-bed,
Copper, orange, all aglow,
Making such a stately show.

I, their fairy, say Good-bye,
For the last of all am I.
Now the Alphabet is said
All the way from A to Z.

Zinnia

Also by Cicely Mary Barker

Flower Fairies of the Spring
Flower Fairies of the Summer
Flower Fairies of the Autumn
Flower Fairies of the Winter
Flower Fairies of the Trees
Flower Fairies of the Garden
Flower Fairies of the Wayside